E $8.95
Al   Alexander, Liza
              I want to go to
           school too

DATE DUE

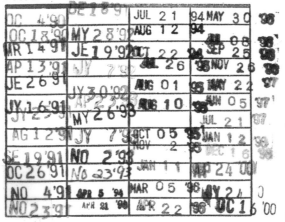

	DE 18 '89	JUL 21	94 MAY 30	'96
OC 4 '90	MY 28 '90	AUG 12	94	
OC 18 '90			JL 08	'96
MR 14 '91	JE 19 '92	OCT 22	94 SEP 25	'96
AP 13 '91	JY 7 '92	JL 26	95 NOV 26	'96
JE 26 '91		AUG 01	95 MAY 22	'97
	JY 30 '92	JL 10	95 JUN 05	'97
JY 16 '91	AP 22 '93			
JY 23 '91	MY 26 '93		JUL 21	'97
AG 12 '91	JY 7 '93	OCT 05	95 JAN 12	'98
		NOV 2	95 DEC 16	'98
SE 19 '91	NO 2 '93	JAN 11		
OC 26 '91	NO 23 '93		AP 24 00	
NO 4 '91	APR 5 '94	MAR 05	'96 MY 24	0
NO 23 '91	APR 21 '94	APR 22	96 OC 16	'00

DEMCO

I Want to Go to School Too

By Liza Alexander
Illustrated by Joe Ewers

A SESAME STREET/GOLDEN PRESS BOOK

Published by Western Publishing Company, Inc.,
in conjunction with Children's Television Workshop

This year my big brother, Herry, is going to
kindergarten. I want to go to school too.

Before Herry's first day of school, Mommy took us shopping. Herry got his first pair of school shoes. I got a new pair of sneakers, but I've had sneakers since I was a baby.

Herry got six yellow pencils and an eraser. He also got a schoolbag. I got crayons and two coloring books, but I already know how to color.

One day we picked up Herry at school. We went to
the supermarket and Herry's teacher was there! I got
to meet her. Her name is Miss Plum. She's very pretty
and she laughs a lot. She teaches the children
different things. I wish I had my own teacher just
like Miss Plum.

Every day I wait for Herry to come home. I always ask him what he did in school that day. Some days he tells me.

My big brother says that at school he has his own
hook and his own cubby. Every morning when Herry
gets to school, he hangs up his coat. Then he puts his
schoolbag in his cubby.

Herry can keep anything he wants in his cubby. That's where he kept our bird's nest. He brought it for show-and-tell. Herry told the children and Miss Plum how we found it on the ground after a thunderstorm. He told them that I helped find it. I want to go to show-and-tell too!

In kindergarten Herry is learning his ABC's. He can almost write all the letters of the alphabet by himself. He uses one of his new pencils. Sometimes he makes a mistake. Then he writes the letter again until he thinks it looks right.

Herry learned the alphabet song at school. He taught me how to sing it. It goes like this:

A B C D E F G
H I J K L M N O
P Q R S
T U V W
X Y Z

Sometimes Miss Plum reads the children a story. Herry tells me the stories when he comes home. My favorite is the one where the shoe fits the girl and she becomes a princess and gets to ride in a pumpkin carriage.

They have quiet time at school every day. The children spread their blankets on the floor and shut their eyes for a nap.

I spread my quilt on the floor and take a nap at home just like my big brother does at school.

One day it was Herry's job to feed the fish. Miss Plum showed him how to give the fish just a tiny bit of food so they don't eat too much. Herry was very careful. He sprinkled just the right amount of food into the fish tank.

Herry says they always play music and sing songs at school.

He taught me how to sing "Twinkle, Twinkle,
Little Star." It goes like this:

Twinkle, twinkle, little star,
How I wonder what you are,
Up above the world so high,
Like a diamond in the sky.

In kindergarten my big brother is learning to count to 100! He can already count up to 23. Herry helped me count my crayons. I have 20.

They have art in school. Herry made me a picture
for my birthday. He cut out some shapes with his
scissors. Then he pasted them on a piece of paper.

Herry told me the names of the shapes in the picture. Here's what they are called:

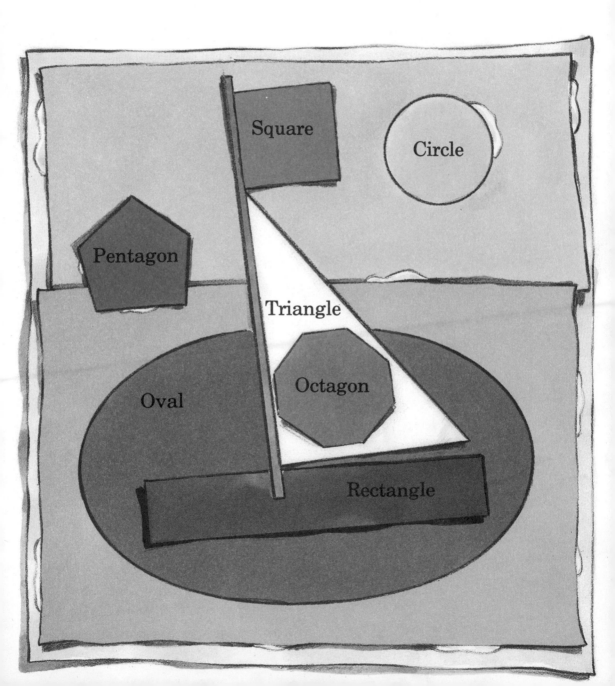

Every day at school the children have playtime.
Herry says they have a huge box of blocks right in
the kindergarten room. They have more blocks at
school than we have at home. Sometimes Herry and
his friends make a great big castle with all their
blocks.

They have toys at school too. Sometimes Herry
plays dolls with Betty Lou. Sometimes he plays dump
truck with Grover.

If it's sunny, Herry's class plays outside.

Sometimes the children play Duck, Duck, Goose. I asked my big brother, Herry, to play Duck, Duck, Goose with me at home. He said two monsters weren't enough to play. I want to play Duck, Duck, Goose too!

Every morning at school the children have snack time. They drink juice out of little paper cups and eat graham crackers. They can have seconds if they want.

Sometimes Herry helps clean up after snack time.
He picks up all the trash and then he throws it into
the trash can.

I asked my mommy if I could have snack time at
home too. Now I eat graham crackers and drink juice
in a little paper cup just like Herry does at school.

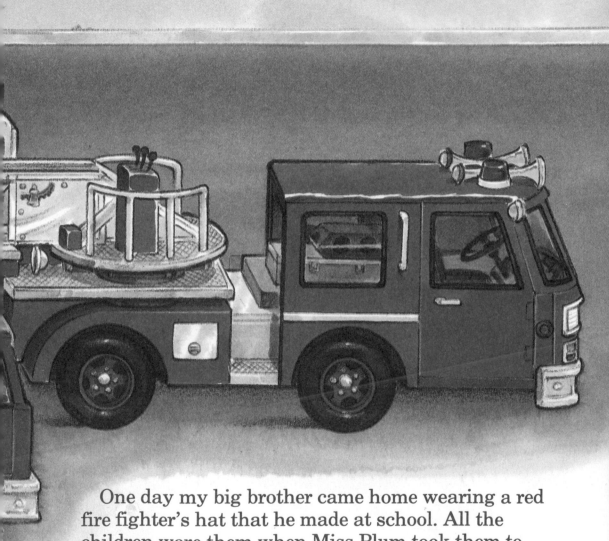

One day my big brother came home wearing a red
fire fighter's hat that he made at school. All the
children wore them when Miss Plum took them to
visit the firehouse. They wore name tags and had
buddies. Herry's buddy was Betty Lou. They saw fire
engines and talked to a real fire fighter.

I want a hat like that!

My big brother, Herry, is lucky that he goes to school. My mommy says I can go to kindergarten when I'm five. I wish I were five now. I want to go to school too!